T0151056

NOTES ON THOUGHT AND VISION
& THE WISE SAPPHO

NOTES ON THOUGHT AND VISION
& THE WISE SAPPHO

By H.D.

City Lights Books
San Francisco

"The Thistle and the Serpent," by Albert Gelpi.
Copyright © 1982 by Albert Gelpi

Published by permission of The Beinecke Rare Book and Manuscript Library, Yale University.

Grateful acknowledgement is made to Perdita Schaffner; James Laughlin of New Directions; Martha Rodgers of Polis; and David E. Schoonover, Curator, American Literature Collection, Beinecke Rare Book and Manuscript Library, Yale University.

Editing and glossary by Anne Janowitz
Cover design by Rex Ray

Library of Congress Cataloging-in-Publication Data:

H.D. (Doolittle, Hilda). 1886-1961.
  Notes on thought and vision.
  I. Title
  PS3507.0726n6   1982   801'92   82-17903
  ISBN: 0-87286-142-4 (pbk)

Visit us on the web at: **www.citylights.com**

CITY LIGHTS BOOKS are edited by Lawrence Ferlinghetti and Nancy J. Peters and published at the City Lights Bookstore, 261 Columbus Avenue, San Francisco, CA 94133.

CONTENTS

Introduction:
Notes on Thought and Vision

THE THISTLE AND THE SERPENT
Albert Gelpi

The inscriptions "July, Scilly Islands," on the manuscript of "Notes on Thought and Vision" locate this puzzling notebook and the transforming event embodied in it. 1919 marked the turning point in H.D.'s life. The previous years had been a period so filled with both achievement and anxiety, so critical and traumatic that she would spend the rest of her life mythologizing it: rehearsing it in verse, in prose, in direct autobiography and in historical and legendary personae, again and again seeking to unriddle her destiny as woman and poet.

She came to the Scilly Islands off the Cornwall coast with her young friend Bryher who had, she felt, given her the will to live when she lay in despair near death. There, Bryher hoped, H.D. might rest in the haven of her devotion and be healed by the wild sea and air—rest and rise again from the wreckage of the previous five years. H.D. found herself, in every respect, *in extremis* on unknown boundaries and strange thresholds. At this crosspoint she was peculiarly and vulnerably liminal: subject to influences and manifestations which consciousness usually ignores or represses. Off Land's End she had what she would call in the "Notes" her "jellyfish experience."

She was undergoing a severe psychic breakdown and her extreme sensitivity had made her preternaturally susceptible to the intensities of experience others might overlook. The *Sea Garden* poems, published to great acclaim in 1916, made her readers feel the cut of wind, the pressure of heat, the sting of sand-grains. In the poems of "Hilda's Book," Ezra Pound loved her as his "Dryad" or tree-sprite initiating him into the mysteries of the vital cosmos. William Carlos Williams had watched stunned once when she was caught up, enraptured, in a thunderstorm and on another occasion when she waded out into pounding surf until it beat her senseless. But this "jellyfish experience" was somewhat different, and more unsettling. It followed personal loss and public catastrophe and it was to be followed by other moments of special release and even revelation: the paradisal vision aboard ship in Greece with the mysterious Peter van Eck at railside with her when the sea-surge seemed suddenly to move in rhythm with a cosmic harmony; the cryptic "writing on the wall" in the hotel room in Corfu, which Freud would later help her construe; the visitations from the magnificent Lady and the apparition of the flowering tree in the London blitz which generated the war *Trilogy;* not to mention the countless dreams, spectral moments, and seances recorded in her voluminous journals and published works.

She knew all too well the dangers in her psychic vulnerability to periodic breakdowns, but her unusual susceptibility also made possible a breakthrough into heightened consciousness. The importance of "Notes on Thought and Vision" is that it anticipates a lifetime spent in the divination of such epiphanal "spots of time."

But what had brought H.D. to the Scillies in 1919 and to the "jellyfish experience"? When, as arrestingly beautiful Hilda Doolittle, she had come to Europe in 1911, she had distanced herself from her family in Philadelphia and her ambivalent feelings about her parents. But she had not left behind youthful attachments to Ezra Pound and Francis Joseph Gregg. She had gone abroad with Francis and become part of Pound's literary circle in London. (These early attachments are recounted in *End to Torment* and *HERmione*.) H.D. was disappointed when Pound broke their vague Philadelphia engagement and married Dorothy Shakespear, but she found compensation in being accepted as a serious poet by Pound and his coterie, notably the handsome, passionate Richard Aldington, with whom she shared manuscripts and professional encouragement.

Pound got her published in *Poetry* as "H.D. Imagiste" in January, 1913. She married Aldington in October of that year, and they were happy the first few years of their marriage, occupied with their own work and editing the Imagist anthologies with Amy Lowell. But the headiness of this time was short-lived. The War drew them all into its madness

and destroyed their fragile world. In 1915 H.D. lost
a daughter through a miscarriage precipitated, she
was convinced, by her grief at the sinking of the
Lusitania. Aldington enlisted in 1916 and was sent
to the French front not long after. On leaves home,
he vainly sought to exorcise his obsession with
impending death through compulsive sexual affairs
that wounded H.D. deeply and convinced her that
he must be shell-shocked. Their time together then
became a torment for both and brought their marriage to the brink of disintegration.

Bid Me To Live associates the breakup of the
marriage with the abrupt end of her spiritual passion for D.H. Lawrence during the winter of 1917-
18 when he and Frieda were sharing the Aldingtons'
flat. With Aldington's assent H.D. went to Cornwall with the musician Cecil Gray, on the understanding that she and Richard would take up their
damaged marriage after the war. However, when
H.D. became pregnant with Gray's child, Aldington
wavered, furious at first and then agreeing to accept
her and the child. But then he abandoned her after
all, declaring himself unable to leave his mistress
and threatening H.D. with prison if she gave the
child his name.

Death stalked her in the closing months and
the aftermath of the War. Her brother Gilbert was
killed in France. Her grief-stricken father died in
February, 1919, when H.D. was about to give birth.
Overwhelmed herself, H.D. contracted the
influenza which seemed like a post-war plague. She
found herself utterly alone in a seedy boarding

house, with doctors predicting that mother and child would not both survive. Fevered and desperate, H.D. awaited birth and death. Then, miraculously, Bryher arrived, pledging her love and her determination that both mother and child would survive. When Francis Perdita was born on March 31, 1919, both did survive. Now, only two months later, the two women and the baby took refuge on the Scilly Islands, where H.D. could recover her strength to go to Greece for the first time. The survivor stood uncertainly between the wreckage behind her and whatever might lie ahead.

It would be melodrama if it were not biography. And there, at this crucial point, with the woman who had mothered her and the child she had borne, she moved into moments of consciousness in which feelings of separateness gave way to a sense of organic wholeness: collapse gave way to coherence and alienation to participation in a cosmic scheme. It would be a characteristic pattern in her life, defining the pattern of her writing: paradisal vision subsuming the abysmal darkness. The necessity to reconcile her agonized experience of contradictions and her intimations of transcendance led her to seek scientific explanations in Freudian analysis and occult explanations in myth, spiritualism, and hermetic cults.

In "Notes on Thought and Vision," she had already grasped, in a somewhat inchoate mixture of seemingly rational discriminations and mythic invocations, the essential ideas she would come to express more profoundly in the great sequence of her late years: *Trilogy, Helen in Egypt, Hermetic Definition.* "Notes" is filled with dualisms that seem to split experience at all levels: body and spirit, womb and head, feeling and thought, the unconscious and ego consciousness, female and male, nature and divinity, classical and Christian, Greek and Hebrew, Greek and Egyptian, Sphinx and Centaur, Pan and Helios, Naiads and Athene, thistle and serpent. But the impulse behind "Notes" is to account for those mysterious moments in which the polarities seemed to fall away, or—more accurately—to find their contradictions lifted and subsumed into a gestalt that illuminated the crosspatch of the past and released her to the chances of the future. At such times H.D. felt delivered from the stresses of the quotidian into a state which she described in metaphor as a kind of lens or a transparent cap of water or envelopment by "a closed sea-plant, jellyfish or anemone."

"Over-mind" has a Nietzschean, elitist ring, but it is, at least theoretically, "there for everyone," however few actually aspire to attain it. And if it also sounds like Emerson's Oversoul, its more immediate source is the Moravian pietism of H.D.'s mother's family. Freud would not have put much credence in such notions, and indeed H.D.'s belief in the transcendental is the locus of her later differences with him. But Jung would have been sympathetic to her experience of an over-mind that allows a sense of participation in both the natural and the transcendental and a perception of "eternal, changeless ideas"; and he would have agreed that through the over-mind the individual can "complete himself" and realize what his nature shares in common with others. At such moments, she could be Greek and Egyptian, pagan and Galilean, womb and head, thistle and serpent.

Jelly-fish consciousness, then, was no disembodied state of neoplatonist abstraction. H.D. had recently come to know Havelock Ellis, but even earlier Pound and Lawrence had argued that sexuality and spirituality were inseparable. And so the over-consciousness envelops the body, the jellyfish tentacles extending not only down from the head but also up from the "love-region." Unencumbered by the misogynist phallicism of Pound and Lawrence, H.D. experienced over-consciousness as "vision of the womb" complementing their phallic enlightenment. Through womb-vision she might give birth to herself, perhaps had begun to do so. No wonder she associated the jellyfish experience with her survival after bearing her child.

H.D.'s signet was the thistle and the serpent, not separate and antagonistic, but paired. The thistle is life accepted in the knowledge of death, "pain and despair." Just as life is inseparable from death, so death metamorphoses "the stings of life" into immortality. The serpent "has symbolised in all ages" death translated into the possibility of "highest life," and H.D. wrote, "in my personal language or vision, I call this serpent a jelly-fish." Resurrection, here and now, through "the serpent—the jellyfish—the overconscious mind." Moreover, "the realisation of this over-conscious mind is the concern of the artist," especially.

The image of the thistle and the serpent, in their essential contradiction and connection, had come to her in a dream when she was eighteen or nineteen. Pound, in Philadelphia, had unsatisfactorily tried to interpret the serpent for her, but did not take up the thistle at all. On her first trip to Europe in 1911, H.D. stood transfixed but not disbelieving before a glass case in the Louvre which contained on exhibit unique among the hundreds of others: a signet-ring incised with the thistle and serpent. She would talk to Freud about the configuration, but already, in 1919 on the Scilly Islands, she knew what it symbolized, and knew too that it was her signet.

Notes on Thought and Vision

Scilly Islands
July 1919

Three states or manifestations of life: body, mind, over-mind.

Aim of men and women of highest development is equilibrium, balance, growth of the three at once; brain without physical strength is a manifestation of weakness, a disease comparable to cancerous growth or tumor; body without reasonable amount of intellect is an empty fibrous bundle of glands as ugly and little to be desired as body of a victim of some form of elephantiasis or fatty-degeneracy; over-mind without the balance of the other two is madness and a person so developed should have as much respect as a reasonable maniac and no more.

○

All reasoning, normal, sane and balanced men and women need and seek at certain times of their lives, certain definite physical relationships. Men and women of temperament, musicians, scientists, artists especially, need these relationships to develop and draw forth their talents. Not to desire and make every effort to develop along these natural physical lines, cripples and dwarfs the being. To shun, deny and belittle such experiences is to bury one's talent carefully in a napkin.

○

When a creative scientist, artist or philosopher has been for some hours or days intent on his work, his mind often takes on an almost physical character. That is, his mind becomes his real body. His over-mind becomes his brain.

When Leonardo da Vinci worked, his brain was Leonardo, the personality, Leonardo da Vinci. He saw the faces of many of his youths and babies and young women definitely with his over-mind. The *Madonna of the Rocks* is not a picture. It is a window. We look through a window into the world of pure over-mind.

○

If I could visualise or describe that over-mind in my own case, I should say this: it seems to me that a cap is over my head, a cap of consciousness over my head, my forehead, affecting a little my eyes. Sometimes when I am in that state of consciousness, things about me appear slightly blurred as if seen under water.

Ordinary things never become quite unreal nor disproportionate. It is only an effort to readjust, to focus, seemingly a slight physical effort.

○

That over-mind seems a cap, like water, transparent, fluid yet with definite body, con-

tained in a definite space. It is like a closed
sea-plant, jelly-fish or anemone.

Into that over-mind, thoughts pass and
are visible like fish swimming under clear
water.

O

The swing from normal consciousness to
abnormal consciousness is accompanied by
grinding discomfort of mental agony.

O

I should say—to continue this jelly-fish
metaphor—that long feelers reached down and
through the body, that these stood in the same
relation to the nervous system as the over-mind
to the brain or intellect.

There is, then, a set of super-feelings.
These feelings extend out and about us; as the
long, floating tentacles of the jelly-fish reach
out and about him. They are not of different
material, extraneous, as the physical arms and
legs are extraneous to the gray matter of the
directing brain. The super-feelers are part of
the super-mind, as the jelly-fish feelers are the
jelly-fish itself, elongated in fine threads.

I first realised this state of consciousness
in my head. I visualise it just as well, now,
centered in the love-region of the body or
placed like a foetus in the body.

The centre of consciousness is either the brain or the love-region of the body.

○

Is it easier for a woman to attain this state of consciousness than for a man?

For me, it was before the birth of my child that the jelly-fish conciousness seemed to come definitely into the field or realm of the intellect or brain.

○

Are these jelly-fish states of consciousness interchangeable? Should we be able to think with the womb and feel with the brain?

May this consciousness be centered entirely in the brain or entirely in the womb or corresponding love-region of a man's body?

○

Vision is of two kinds—vision of the womb and vision of the brain. In vision of the brain, the region of consciousness is above and about the head; when the centre of consciousness shifts and the jelly-fish is in the body, (I visualise it in my case lying on the left side with the streamers or feelers floating up toward the brain) we have vision of the womb or love-vision.

○

The majority of dream and of ordinary vision is vision of the womb.

The brain and the womb are both centres of consciousness, equally important.

○

Most of the so-called artists of today have lost the use of their brain. There is no way of arriving at the over-mind, except through the intellect. To arrive at the world of over-mind vision any other way, is to be the thief that climbs into the sheep-fold.

I believe there are artists coming in the next generation, some of whom will have the secret of using their over-minds.

○

Over-mind artists usually come in a group. There were the great Italians: Verrochio, Angelo, Ghiberti, the lot that preceded and followed da Vinci, including statesmen, explorers, and men and women of curious and sensitive development.

There was the great Athenian group: the dramatists, Socrates, the craftsmen and the men and women, their followers and lovers.

○

There is no great art period without great lovers.

O

Socrates' whole doctrine of vision was a doctrine of love.

We must be "in love" before we can understand the mysteries of vision.

A lover must choose one of the same type of mind as himself, a musician, a musician, a scientist, a scientist, a general, a young man also interested in the theory and practice of arms and armies.

We begin with sympathy of thought. The minds of the two lovers merge, interact in sympathy of thought.

The brain, inflamed and excited by this interchange of ideas, takes on its character of over-mind, becomes (as I have visualised in my own case) a jelly-fish, placed over and about the brain.

The love-region is excited by the appearance or beauty of the loved one, its energy not dissipated in physical relation, takes on its character of mind, becomes this womb-brain or love-brain that I have visualised as a jelly-fish *in* the body.

The love-brain and over-brain are both capable of thought. This thought is vision.

O

All men have possibilities of developing this vision.

The over-mind is like a lens of an opera-glass. When we are able to use this over-mind lens, the whole world of vision is open to us.

I have said that the over-mind is a lens. I should say more exactly that the love-mind and the over-mind are two lenses. When these lenses are properly adjusted, focused, they bring the world of vision into consciousness. The two work separately, perceive separately, yet make one picture.

○

The mystic, the philosopher is content to contemplate, to examine these pictures. The Attic dramatist reproduced them for men of lesser or other gifts. He realised, the whole time, that they were not his ideas. They were eternal, changeless ideas that he had grown aware of, dramas already conceived that he had watched; memory is the mother, begetter of all drama, idea, music, science or song.

○

We may enter the world of over-mind consciousness directly, through the use of our over-mind brain. We may enter it indirectly, in various ways. Every person must work out his own way.

Certain words and lines of Attic choruses, any scrap of da Vinci's drawings, the Delphic charioteer, have a definite, hypnotic effect on me. They are straight, clear entrances, to me, to over-world consciousness. But my line of approach, my sign-posts, are not your sign-posts.

○

My sign-posts are not yours, but if I blaze my own trail, it may help to give you confidence and urge you to get out of the murky, dead, old, thousand-times explored old world, the dead world of overworked emotions and thoughts.

But the world of the great creative artists is never dead. The new schools of destructive art theorists are on the wrong track. Because Leonardo and his kind are never old, never dead. Their world is never explored, hardly even entered. Because it needs an over-mind or a slight glimmering of over-mind intelligence to understand over-mind intelligence.

○

The Delphic charioteer has, I have said, an almost hypnotic effect on me: the bend of his arm, the knife-cut of his chin; his feet, rather flat, slightly separated, a firm pedestal for himself; the fall of his drapery, in geometri-

Charioteer at Delphi

cal precision; and the angles of the ingatherings of the drapery at the waist.

All this was no "inspiration," it was sheer, hard brain work.

This figure has been created by a formula arrived at consciously or unconsciously.

If we had the right sort of brains, we would receive a definite message from that figure, like dots and lines ticked off by one receiving station, received and translated into definite thought by another telegraphic centre.

There is no trouble about art. There is already enough beauty in the world of art, enough in the fragments and the almost perfectly preserved charioteer at Delphi alone to remake the world.

There is no trouble about the art, it is the appreciators we want. We want young men and women to communicate with the charioteer and his like.

We want receiving centres for dots and dashes.

○

It is said that da Vinci went mad if he saw a boy's face in Florence or a caged bird or a child with yellow hair that fell or stood up in tight whorls like the goldsmith work he had learned with Verrochio. Da Vinci went mad because those lines of the bird's back or the boy's shoulder or the child's hair acted on him directly, as the lines of a statue, worked out like the charioteer, would act on us if we had the right sort of receiving brain.

○

Two or three people, with healthy bodies and the right sort of receiving brains, could turn the whole tide of human thought, could direct lightning flashes of electric power to slash across and destroy the world of dead, murky thought.

Two or three people gathered together in the name of truth, beauty, over-mind consciousness could bring the whole force of this power back into the world.

○

It is true that, in the year A.D.361, the Galilean conquered at Delphi. That was because the Hellenic mind had entirely lost the secret of dots and dashes. The electric force of the lines and angles of the priest-like body of the charioteer still gave out their message but there was no one to receive this message.

The Galilean conquered because he was a great artist, like da Vinci.

A fish-basket, upturned on the sand, or a candle in a candle-stick or a Roman coin with its not unbeautifully wrought head of a king, could excite him and give him ideas, as the bird or boy's face or child's yellow hair gave da Vinci ideas.

○

The Galilean fell in love with things as well as people. He would fall in love with a sea-gull or some lake-heron that would dart up from the coarse lake grass, when Peter leapt out to drag his great boat on shore, or the plain little speckled-backed birds bought in the market by the poor Jews. Then, he would look at Peter with his great archaic head and the young Jude with his intense eyes, and he would exclaim suddenly: "Ah, but your faces, your faces are more beautiful, more charged with ideas, with lines that suggest and bring me into touch with the world of over-mind thought, than many, many sparrows."

○

He looked at the blue grass-lily and the red-brown sand-lily that grew under the sheltered hot sand-banks in the southern winter, for hours and hours. If he closed his eyes, he saw every vein and fleck of blue or vermilion. He would breathe in the fragrance with the wind and the salt. He would rest for days along the shores of the sea-lakes.

Then, in the town, there would be some tragedy and he would send the friends and wailing relatives out of the way. He would be angry, as he looked at the little girl's face, that she was surrounded by such ugliness. He would look at her for a long time because of the beauty of the little, straight nose and the eyelids, the hair clinging like seaweed to the fine little skull, the very white hands. He would like to have stayed looking at her for hours, like the blue grass-lily. But he was afraid they would break in, suddenly again, with their heavy, black clothes, and ugly voices. So he said, "Daughter, I say unto you, arise."

○

The first step in the Eleusinian mysteries had to do with sex. There were images set up in a great room, coloured marbles and brown pottery, painted with red and vermilion and coloured earthen work or clay images. The candidates for admission to the mysteries would be shown through the room by a priest or would walk through at random, as the crowd walks through the pornographic chamber at the museum at Naples.

It would be easy enough to judge them by their attitude, whether it was one of crude animal enjoyment or hypocritical aloofness.

The crowd that got through to the second room would be different, more sensitive, more fastidious. They would correspond to certain of our intellectual types of today. They would be interested because it was the thing to be interested—also to show their superiority.

Any one who got safely through the mere animal stage and the intellectual stage would be left in a small room by himself to make his constatation.

○

Anyone who wants can get through these stages today just as easily as the Eleusinian candidates outside Athens in the fifth century, B.C.

There is plenty of pornographic literature that is interesting and amusing.

If you cannot be entertained and instructed by Boccaccio, Rabelais, Montaigne, Sterne, Middleton, de Gourmont and de Régnier there is something wrong with you physically.

If you cannot read these people and enjoy them you are not ready for the first stage of initiation.

○

If you do read these people and enjoy them and enjoy them really with your body, because you have a normal healthy body, then you may be ready for the second stage of initiation.

You can look into things with your intellect, with your sheer brain.

○

If your brain cannot stand the strain of following out these lines of thought, scientifically, and if you are not balanced and sane enough to grasp these things with a certain amount of detachment, you are obviously not ready for experiments in over-mind consciousness.

○

Socrates said, "There are many wand-bearers but few inspired." He meant, by wand-bearers, people who had passed the first two stages of the Eleusinian mysteries. We mean by wand-bearers today, intelligent people of normal development, who have looked into matters of life scientifically and with a certain amount of artistic appreciation.

Today there are many wand-bearers but few inspired.

○

One must understand a lower wisdom before one understands a higher. One must understand Euripides before one understands

Aristophanes. Yet to understand dung chemically and spiritually and with the earth sense, one must first understand the texture, spiritual and chemical and earthy, of the rose that grows from it.

Euripides is a white rose, lyric, feminine, a spirit. Aristophanes is a satyr.

Is the satyr greater or less than the white rose it embraces? Is the earth greater or less than the white rose it brings forth? Is the dung greater or less than the rose?

○

Flowers are made to seduce the senses: fragrance, form, colour.

If you can not be seduced by beauty, you cannot learn the wisdom of ugliness.

○

Zeus Endendros—God in a tree; Dionysius Anthios, God in a flower; Zeus Melios, God in the black earth, death, disruption, disintegration; Dionysius Zagreus, the flower torn, broken by chemical process of death, vein, leaf, texture—white luminous lily surface, veined with black—white lily flesh bruised, withered. "I, Lais, place my mirror here at thy feet, O Paphian—I remember and I dare not remember. Is there a mystery beyond that of thy white arms, O Aphrogenia? Is there

a beauty greater than the white pear-branch
which broke so white against a black April
storm sky that Zeus himself was roused from
his sacred meditation, as from the ranges of
Olympos he gazed below upon the Attic pas-
tures. He gazed below and saw you, O white
branch. He was angry, for you were more white
against the sky than the passion of his shaft.
For that reason he sent lightning to blast you,
O tree. Since then no man may speak your
name, O Goddess. But we know there is a
mystery greater than beauty and that is death."

O

The heat, the stench of things, the unutter-
able boredom of it all, Meleager of Gadara,
what a fate; a Jew father, a Greek mother.
What God of the Hebrew, what demon of the
islands had presided at his ill-omened begetting? Heliodora, Zenophile, what were they but
names? Greek prostitutes—branded by Syrian
traders and Jew merchants alike. The stench—
the dust, Meleager of Gadara—what a fate.

No wind and the sea stretching like the
dead parchment rent with the devil tokens—
the Hebrew script he would die to forget—the
tongue he would die to forget—but that in
dying he would forget that other—gold—light
of gold—words, potent, a charm each leading
to a world where there were cold flowers.

Heliodora, Zenophile—no Attic hetairas.

Flowers?

The roses that he had touched that morning—the boy at the wharf pier—he had stepped from a boat, wet with the sea about the islands. But the boy's wet curls smelt of salt fish and his roses were already rank—rotting—and he had dipped their streaked stems in cheap myrrh to cheat the Heliodoras of this world of their sparse [...]

Gods, dead alike of Greek and Hebrew. What devil had sent a swine, a pig to plant its two feet on his door step and gaze within? Voices and shouting. He would never find peace that day for the golden branch of the divine Plate ever shining by its own light.

A pig on the door step.

To live with a poet's mind in a slum of Gadara. Meleager—what daemon of the islands was present at your ill-omened begetting?

To live with a poet's mind in a slum of Gadara or to live with princely Jews his father's friend—a merchant respected—his father again—in the palaces of Syrian princes.

There was no choice—*but a pig on the door step.*

Avaunt pig! Must I sacrifice the script of the golden Plate to hurl at that pig?

After all, could the script of the golden high falutin' high-sounding Plate be put to a better use?

He ignores the script, save to turn it over with his snout. What devil possesses him?

Well, here is my Gadarene foot then.

A herd of them in the street.

Beyond the stifling dust, someone is shouting. A voice, more portent than the script of the golden Plate. Speaking Greek too.

"Be you entered into the sea."

Praise every god of Greek or Hebrew they are gone.

A crowd of the usual slum vandals—and one young man who is laughing.

○

A princely stranger and his father, a Jew too. What cool hands at parting.

Beyond the Zenophiles of this world there is another Zenophile, beyond the Heliodoras another Heliodora, beyond the dank, hot and withering roses, other roses.

A princely stranger and a poet.

I would make him some gift, for his brow was more lordly (though his father was no Greek) than the Kyllenian Hermes.

The Muse Terpsichore. The Peleus Painter, 440 B.C.

I would bind narcissus to narcissus. I would plait the red violet to the white violet. I would break for you one rose, more red than the wine-cyclamen. I would bind the stem of the crocus to the stem of the wild-hyacinth, that each might show less lovely about your brow, Kyllenian Hermes.

○

Egypt in the terms of world-consciousness is the act of love. Hellas is a child born.

The secret of the Sphinx is the secret of knowledge. The secret of the Centaur is the secret of feeling.

The Sphinx knows everything. The Centaur feels everything.

○

Three worlds.
1. World of abstraction: Helios, Athene.
2. Intermediate or Nature world: Pan, the Naiads.
3. World of the uninitiate men and women.

All these worlds are important, equally important. But we are important only insofar as we become identified with the highest in ourselves—"our own familiar daemon."

○

Spirits of a higher world have access into a lower world. Athene may appear to one in the next lower world. She may be the companion of a half-god, but she must preserve her dignity, her Olympian character. Athene perfectly did this. Therefore the gods accepted and enrolled Odysseus among the half-gods and heroes.

But when there was a question of Artemis losing caste by her association with the too boorish giant, Orion, the giant was slain.

However, lest honour should be lacking the Olympian hierarchy because of this lapse of taste, Orion was afterwards received among the stars.

O

It was *de rigueur* for an Olympian not to appear to a mortal direct. Therefore Selene who requested this, was burned to ash.

But we have many records of Naiads, tree and river spirits, sea spirits and voices of the sea, and Centaurs holding friendly intercourse with mortals.

We also know that Pan appeared to those in pain or trouble, not only in dreams but "visibly at mid-day."

Pan appeared at Marathon before all the Greeks. And I know of witnesses today who have had vision of this god.

○

Normal consciousness, pricks of everyday discomfort, jealousy and despair and various forms of unhappiness that are the invariable accompaniment of any true, deep relationship, all this may be symbolised by a thistle.

There are two ways of escaping the pain and despair of life, and of the rarest, most subtle dangerous and ensnaring gift that life can bring us, relationship with another person—love.

One way is to kill that love in one's heart. To kill love—to kill life.

The other way is to accept that love, to accept the snare, to accept the pricks, the thistle.

To accept life—but that is dangerous.

It is also dangerous not to accept life.

To every man and woman in the world it is given at some time or another, in some form or another, to make the choice.

Every man and woman is free to accept or deny life—to accept or reject this questionable gift—this thistle.

○

But these notes are concerned chiefly with the mental process that is in some form or other the complement of the life process.

That is to say this thistle—life, love, martyrdom—leads in the end—must lead in the logical course of events to death, paradise, peace.

That world of death—that is, death to the stings of life, which is the highest life—may be symbolised by the serpent.

The world of vision has been symbolised in all ages by various priestly cults in all countries by the serpent.

In my personal language or vision, I call this serpent a jelly-fish.

○

The serpent—the jelly-fish—the over-conscious mind.

The realisation of this over-conscious world is the concern of the artist.

But this world is there for everyone.

The minds of men differ but the over-minds are alike.

○

Our minds, all of our minds, are like dull little houses, built more or less alike—a dull little city with rows of little detached villas, and here and there a more pretentious house, set apart from the rest, but in essentials, seen from a distance, one with the rest, all drab, all grey.

Each comfortable little home shelters a comfortable little soul—and a wall at the back shuts out completely any communication with the world beyond.

Man's chief concern is keeping his little house warm and making his little wall strong.

○

Outside is a great vineyard and grapes and rioting and madness and dangers.

It is very dangerous.

An enormous moth detached himself from a bunch of yellow grapes—he seemed stupified with the heat of the sun—heavy with the sun and his soft belly swollen with the honey of the grapes, I would have said, for there was a bead of gold—resinous—that matted the feathers at his throat.

He fell rather than flew and his great feet scratched with a faint metallic ring, the side of my golden cup.

He stumbled, awkward and righted himself, clutched the rim of my cup, waved his antennae feebly.

I would have rescued him but I myself was dizzy with the heat and the fumes of the golden

wine and I heard a great shout of laughter as I
tried to steady my cup and I shouted in reply,
he is drunk—*he* is drunk.

So he was drunk.

Outside is a great vineyard and rioting and
madness and dangers.

○

The body—limbs of a tree, branches of a
fruit-tree, the whole body a tree—philosophy
of the Tao, philosophy of the Hebrew, philosophy of the Greek, man identified with nature,
the just man "a tree planted by the rivers,"
numerous instances of gods in trees and human
beings of peculiar beauty or grace turned at
death, as reward of kindliness, into trees,
poplar trees, mulberry trees, laurels.

But a man has intellect, brain—a mind in
fact, capable of three states of being, a mind
that may be conscious in the ordinary, schol-
arly, literal sense of the word, or sub-
conscious—those sub-conscious states varying
in different states of dream or physical feeling,
or illness, delirium or madness—a mind, over-
conscious as well, able to enter into a whole life
as Leonardo entered, Euripides, the Galilean
with his baskets and men's faces and Roman
coins—the forest hermits of the Ganges and the
painter who concentrated on one tuft of pine
branch with its brown cone until every needle

was a separate entity to him and every pine
needle bore to every other one, a clear relationship like a drawing of a later mechanical twen-
tieth century bridge-builder.

○

Lo-fu sat in his orchard in the Ming dynasty, A.D.184. He sat in his orchard and
looked about in a vague, casual way. Against
the grey stones of the orchard wall he saw the
low branch of an apple tree. He thought, that
shoot should have been pruned, it hangs too
low. Then as he looked at the straight tough
young shoot, he thought, no, the apples are
excellent, so round and firm. Then he went on
looking.

It was a shoot of some years' growth. Why
had it been left untrimmed? Was it some special
experiment in grafting the old gardener had
undertaken some years ago? Was it by accident
that the limb hung there? Then his conscious
mind ceased wondering and, being an artist, his
intensity and concentration were of a special
order and he looked at that fruit branch hang-
ing in the sun, the globes of the apples red,
yellow, red with flecks of brown and red, yellow where the two colours merged, and flecks
of brown again on the yellow, and green as the
round surface curved in toward the stem. He
saw the stem, pushed down almost lost in the
green hollow. He saw the stem fastened to the

tough little branch above. He saw the green brown bark of the stem and he compared it with the darker, stronger bark of the branch. He examined the ridges and the minute black lines that made up the individual surface of that little branch. He went further. There were two leaves, continents to be explored in a leisurely manner lest his mind passing one carelessly from vein to vein, should miss one rib or the small branch of one off-shoot of that exquisite skeleton. And when he knew the skeleton of that leaf, the rivers, as it were, furrowing that continent, his mind was content. But it had only begun its search. Between each river there lay a fair green field—many, many little fields each with an individuality, each with some definite feature setting it apart from every other little plot.

○

I have tried to tell in a small way with as little detail as possible, how Lo-fu looked at that branch. He really did look at it. He really did see it. Then he went inside and in his little cool room out of the sun he closed his eyes. He saw that branch but more clearly, more vividly than ever. That branch was his mistress now, his love. As he saw it in the orchard, that mistress was, as it were, observed in a crowd, from a distance. He could not touch her, his mistress with all the world about. Here, in his little room, the world had ceased to exist. It was shut off, shut out, forgotten. His love, his apple branch, his beautiful subtle mistress, was his. And having possessed her with his great and famished soul, she was his forever.

○

She was his, and though he knew she was only one, one of a thousand women, one of a thousand, thousand, beautiful women, she was his, his own. And he was never jealous, though her beauty was so obvious, for no one else could possess her. Yet unlike another lover, he longed that his friend should love her too, or should make another branch his own, for the orchard was full and beyond the orchard the mountain and pine forests were a thousand intimate friendly herbs and grasses.

Lo-fu was a poet. To him that apple branch, outside in the orchard, existed as an approach to something else. As the body of a man's mistress might be said to exist as the means of approach to something else, that is as a means or instrument of feeling or happiness, so the branch in the orchard existed to Lo-fu as the means of attaining happiness, as a means of completing himself, as a means of approach to ecstasy.

○

I have been talking with a young man, a scholar and philosopher. He says my term over-mind is not good, because in his case at least, the mental state I describe lies below the sub-conscious mind. That is, I visualise my three states of consciousness in a row,

1.   Over-conscious mind.
2.   Conscious mind.
3.   Sub-conscious mind.

He on the other hand visualises his three states,

1.   Conscious mind.
2.   Sub-conscious mind.
3.   Universal mind.

He means by universal mind exactly what I mean by over-mind but certainly my term over-mind is not adequate, if this over-mind state is approached by others through the sub-conscious.

But we both visualise these states in a row, though I suppose the universal symbol is the triangle, or taken a step further, the circle, as the three seem to run into one another, though neither he nor I visualise them that way.

O

The body of a man is a means of approach, or can be used as a means of approach to ecstasy. Man's body can be used for that. The best Greek sculpture used the bodies of young athletes as Lo-fu used the branch of the fruit tree. The lines of the human body may be used as an approach to the over-mind or universal mind.

The lines of the human body and the lines of the fruit tree are like the body of the Delphic charioteer that I spoke of some time ago. The fruit tree and the human body are both receiving stations, capable of storing up energy, over-world energy. That energy·is always there but can be transmitted only to another body or another mind that is in sympathy with it, or keyed to the same pitch.

The body of the Greek boy Polycleitus used for his Diuademenos was as impersonal a thing as a tree. He used the body instead of a tree. That boy's body was, of course, capable of human passions but Polycleitus' approach to that body was not through the human passions.

But of course he was in love with it just as Lo-fu was in love with apple branch and Leonardo with the boy's face or the Galilean with the field lilies.

○

But the body, I suppose, like a lump of coal, fulfills its highest function when it is being consumed.

When coal burns it gives off heat.

The body consumed with love gives off heat.

But taken a step further, coal may be used to make gas, an essence, a concentrated, ethereal form of coal.

So with the body. It may burn out simply as heat or physical love. That may be good. But it is also interesting to understand the process whereby the heat of the physical body is transmuted to this other, this different form, concentrated, ethereal, which we refer to in common speech as spirit.

It is all spirit but spirit in different forms.

We cannot have the heat without the lump of coal.

Perhaps so we cannot have spirit without body, the body of nature, or the body of individual men and women.

○

I spoke to a scientist, a psychologist, about my divisions of mind and over-mind. He said that over-mind was not exactly the right term, that sub-conscious mind was the phrase I was groping for.

I have thought for a long time about the comparative value of these terms, and I see at last my fault and his.

We were both wrong. I was about to cover too much of the field of abnormal consciousness by the term over-mind. He, on the other hand, would have called it all sub-conscious mind.

But the sub-conscious and the over-conscious are entirely different states, entirely different worlds.

○

The sub-conscious world is the world of sleeping dreams and the world great lovers enter, physical lovers, but very great ones.

The over-conscious world is the world of waking dreams and the world great lovers enter, spiritual lovers, but only the greatest.

○

A sub-conscious dream may become an over-conscious dream at the moment of waking.

○

The intellect, the brain, the conscious mind is the bridge across, the link between the sub-conscious and the over-conscious.

I think at last I have my terms clear.

There are three states of manifestations— sub-conscious mind, conscious mind, over-conscious mind.

○

These jelly-fish, I think, are the "seeds cast into the ground." But as it takes a man and woman to create another life, so it takes these two forms of seed, one in the head and one in the body to make a new spiritual birth. I think that is why I saw them as jelly-fish. They are really two flecks of protoplasm and when we are "born again," we begin not as a child but as the very first germs that grow into a child.

○

Probably we pass through all forms of life and that is very interesting. But so far I have passed through these two, I am in my spiritual body a jelly-fish and a pearl.

We can probably use this pearl, as a crystal ball is used, for concentrating and directing pictures from the world of vision.

○

It is necessary to work, to strive toward the understanding of the over-mind. But once a man becomes conscious of this jelly-fish above his head, this pearl within his skull, this seed cast into the ground, his chief concern automatically becomes his body.

Once we become concretely aware of this pearl, this seed, our centre of consciousness shifts. Our concern is with the body.

O

Where does the body come in?

What is the body?

O

I imagine it has often been said that the body is like an oyster and the soul or spirit, a pearl. But today I saw for myself that the jelly-fish over my head had become concentrated. I saw that the state of mind I had before symbolised as a jelly-fish was just as well symbolised differently. That is, all the spiritual energy seemed concentrated in the middle of my forehead, inside my skull, and it was small and giving out a very soft light, but not scattered light, light concentrated in itself as the light of a pearl would be. So I understood exactly what the Galilean meant by the kingdom of heaven, being a pearl of great price.

Then in the same relation, the body was not a very rare or lovely thing. The body seemed an elementary, unbeautiful and transitory form of life. Yet here again, I saw that the body had its use. The oyster makes the pearl in fact. So the body, with all its emotions and fears and pain in time casts off the spirit, a concentrated essence, not itself, but made, in a sense, created by itself.

I know that this has been said before but I speak for myself, from my personal experience.

Because the spirit, we realise, is a seed. No man by thought can add an inch to his stature, no initiate by the strength and power of his intellect can force his spirit to grow.

He cannot force his spirit to grow, but he can retard its growth. At least so it seems to me.

He can retard its growth by neglect of his body because the body of man as the body of nature is the ground into which the seed or spirit is cast.

This is the mystery of Demeter, the Earth Mother. The body of the Eleusinian initiate had become one with the earth, as his soul had become one with the seeds enclosed in the earth.

No man by thought can make the grain sprout or the acorn break its shell. No man by intellectual striving can make his spirit expand.

But every man can till the field, can clear weeds from about the stems of flowers.

Every man can water his own little plot, can strive to quiet down the overwrought tension of his body.

○

Christ and his father, or as the Eleusinian mystic would have said, his mother, were one.

Christ was the grapes that hung against the sun-lit walls of that mountain garden,

Nazareth. He was the white hyacinth of Sparta and the narcissus of the islands. He was the conch shell and the purple-fish left by the lake tides. He was the body of nature, the vine, the Dionysus, as he was the soul of nature.

He was the gulls screaming at low tide and tearing the small crabs from among the knotted weeds.

○

Christ and his father, or as the Eleusinian mystic would have said, his mother, were one.

Christ was the grapes that hung against the sun-lit walls of that mountain garden, Nazareth. He was the white hyacinth of Sparta and the narcissus of the islands. He was the conch shell and the purple-fish left by the lake tides. He was the body of nature, the vine, the Dionysus, as he was the soul of nature.

He was the gulls screaming at low tide and tearing the small crabs from among the knotted weeds.

The Wise Sappho

"Little, but all roses" is the dictate of the Alexandrine poet, yet I am inclined to disagree. I would not bring roses, nor yet the great shaft of scarlet lilies. I would bring orange blossoms, implacable flowerings made to seduce the sense when every other means has failed, poignard that glints, fresh sharpened steel: after the red heart, red lilies, impassioned roses are dead.

"Little, but all roses"—true there is a tint of rich colour (invariably we find it), violets, purple woof of cloth, scarlet garments, dyed fastening of a sandal, the lurid, crushed and perished hyacinth, stains on cloth and flesh and parchment.

There is gold too. Was it a gold rose the poet meant? But the gold of a girl-child's head, the gold of an embroidered garment hem, the rare gold of sea-grass or meadow-pulse does not seem to evoke in our thought the vision of roses, heavy in a scented garden.

"Little, but all roses." I think, though the stains are deep on the red and scarlet cushions, on the flaming cloak of love, it is not warmth we look for in these poems, not fire nor sun-light, not heat in the ordinary sense, diffused, and comforting (nor is it light, day or dawn or light of sun-setting), but another element containing all these, magnetic, vibrant; not the lightning as it falls from the thunder cloud, yet lightning in a sense: white, unhuman element, containing fire and light and warmth, yet in its essence differing from all these, as if the brittle crescent-moon gave heat to us, or some splendid scintillating star turned warm suddenly in our hand like a jewel, sent by the beloved.

I think of the words of Sappho as these colours, or states rather, transcending colour yet containing (as great heat the compass of the spectrum) all colour. And perhaps the most obvious is this rose colour, merging to richer shades of scarlet, purple or Phoenician purple. To the superficial lover—truly—roses!

Yet not all roses—not roses at all, not orange blossoms even, but reading deeper we are inclined to visualize these broken sentences and unfinished rhythms as rocks—perfect rock shelves and layers of rock between which flowers by some chance may grow but which endure when the staunch blossoms have perished.

Not flowers at all, but an island with innumerable, tiny, irregular bays and fjords and little straits between which the sun lies clear (fragments cut from a perfect mirror of iridescent polished silver or of the bronze reflecting richer tints) or breaks, wave upon destructive passionate wave.

Not roses, but an island, a country, a continent, a planet, a world of emotion, differing entirely from any present day imaginable world of emotion; a world of emotion that could only be imagined by the greatest of her own countrymen in the greatest period of that country's glamour, who themselves confessed her beyond their reach, beyond their song, not a woman, not a goddess even, but a song or the spirit of a song.

A song, a spirit, a white star that moves across the heaven to mark the end of a world epoch or to presage some coming glory.

Yet she is embodied—terribly a human being, a woman, a personality as the most impersonal become when they confront their fellow beings.

The under-lip curls out in the white face, she has twisted her two eyes unevenly, the brows break the perfect line of the white forehead, her expression is not exactly sinister (sinister and dead), the spark of mockery beneath the half-closed lids is rather living destructive irony.

"What country girl bewitches your heart who knows not how to draw her skirt about her ankles?"

Aristocratic—indifferent—full of caprice—full of imperfection—intolerant.

High in the mountains, the wind may break the trees, as love the lover, but this was before the days of Theocritus, before the destructive Athenian satyric drama—we hear no praise of country girls nor mountain goats. This woman has still the flawless tradition to maintain.

Her bitterness was on the whole the bitterness of the sweat of Eros. Had she burned to destroy she had spent her flawless talent to destroy custom and mob-thought with serpent-tongue before the great Athenian era.

Black and burnt are the cheeks of the girl
of the late Sicilian Theocritus, for says he,
black is the hyacinth and the myrtle-berry.

But Sappho has no praise for mountain
girls. She protrudes a little her under-lip, twists
her eyes, screws her face out of proportion as
she searches for the most telling phrase; this
girl who bewitches you, my friend, does not
even know how to draw her skirts about her
feet.

Sophisticated, ironical, bitter jeer. Not her
hands, her feet, her hair, or her features resem-
ble in any way those of the country-bred
among the thickets; not her garments even, are
ill-fitting or ill-cut, but her manners, her ges-
tures are crude, the bitterest of all destructive
gibes of one sensitive woman at the favourite of
another, sensitive, high-strung, autocratic as
herself.

The gods, it is true, Aphrodite, Hermes,
Ares, Hephaistos, Adonis, beloved of the
mother of loves, the Graces, Zeus himself, Eros
in all his attributes, great, potent, the Muses,
mythical being and half-god, the Kyprian
again and again are mentioned in these poems
but at the end, it is for the strange almost
petulant little phrases that we value this
woman, this cry (against some simple
unknown girl) of skirts and ankles we might
think unnecessarily petty, yet are pleased in the
thinking of it, or else the outbreak against her
own intimate companions brings her nearer

Portrait of Sappho by Silanion, ca. 350 A.D.
(Imaginary)

our own over-sophisticated, nerve-wracked
era: "The people I help most are the most
unkind," "O you forget me" or "You love
someone better," "You are nothing to me,"
nervous, trivial tirades. Or we have in sweet-
ened mood so simple a phrase "I sing"—not to
please any god, goddess, creed or votary of
religious rite—I sing not even in abstract con-
templation, trance-like, remote from life, to
please myself, but says this most delightful and
friendly woman, "I sing and I sing beautifully
like this, in order to please my friends—my
girl-friends."

We have no definite portraits from her
hands of these young women of Mitylene. They
are left to our imagination, though only the
most ardent heart, the most intense spirit and
the most wary and subtle intellect can hope
even in moments of ardent imagination, to fill
in these broken couplets. One reads simply this
"My darling," or again "You burn me." To a
bride's lover she says, "Ah there never was a
girl like her." She speaks of the light spread
across a lovely face, of the garment wrapped
about a lovely body; she addresses by name
two of these young women comparing one to
another's disadvantage (though even here she
temporizes her judgment with an endearing
adjective), "Mnasidika is more shapely than
tender Gyrinno." We hear of Eranna too.
"Eranna, there never was a girl more spiteful
than you."

Another girl she praises, not for beauty. Though they stand among tall spotted lilies and the cup of jacynth and the Lesbian iris, she yet extolls beyond Kypris and the feet of Eros, wisdom. "Ah," she says of this one, beloved for another beauty than that of perfect waist and throat and close-bound cap of hair and level brows, "I think no girl can ever stand beneath the sun or ever will again and be as wise as you are."

Wisdom—this is all we know of the girl, that though she stood in the heavy Graeco-Asiatic sunlight, the wind from Asia, heavy with ardent myrrh and Persian spices, was yet tempered with a Western gale, bearing in its strength and its salt sting, the image of another, tall, with eyes shadowed by the helmet rim, the goddess, indomitable.

This is her strength—Sappho of Mitylene was a Greek. And in all her ecstasies, her burnings, her Asiatic riot of colour, her cry to that Phoenician deity, "Adonis, Adonis—" her phrases, so simple yet in any but her hands in danger of overpowering sensuousness, her touches of Oriental realism, "purple napkins" and "soft cushions" are yet tempered, moderated by a craft never surpassed in literature. The beauty of Aphrodite it is true is the constant, reiterated subject of her singing. But she is called by a late scholiast who knew more of her than we can hope to learn from these brief fragments, "The Wise Sappho."

We need the testimony of no Alexandrian or late Roman scholiast to assure us of the artistic wisdom, the scientific precision of metre and musical notation, the finely tempered intellect of this woman. Yet for all her artistic moderation, what is the personal, the emotional quality of her wisdom? This woman whom love paralysed till she seemed to herself a dead body yet burnt, as the desert grass is burnt, white by the desert heat; she who trembled and was sick and sweated at the mere presence of another, a person, doubtless of charm, of grace, but of no extraordinary gifts perhaps of mind or feature—was she moderate, was she wise? Savonarola standing in the courtyard of the Medici (some two thousand years later) proclaimed her openly to the assembled youthful laity and priests of Florence—a devil.

If moderation is wisdom, if constancy in love is wisdom, was she wise? We read even in these few existing fragments, name upon curious, exotic, fragrant name: Atthis—Andromeda — Mnasidika — Eranna—Gyrinno—more, many more than these tradition tells were praised in the lost fragments. The name of muse and goddess and of human woman merge, interspersed among these verses. "Niobe and Leda were friends—" it is a simple statement—for the moment, Niobe and Leda are nearer, more human, than the Atthis, the Eranna who strike and burn and break like Love himself.

The wise Sappho! She was wise, emotionally wise, we suspect with wisdom of simplicity, the blindness of genius. She constructed from the simple gesture of a half-grown awkward girl, a being, a companion, an equal. She imagined, for a moment, as the white bird wrinkled a pink foot, clutching to obtain balance at the too smooth ivory of the wrist of the same Atthis, that Atthis had a mind, that Atthis was a goddess. Because the sun made a momentary circlet of strange rust-coloured hair, she saw in all her fragrance, Aphrodite, violet-crowned, or better still a sister, a muse, one of the violet wreathing. She imagined because the girl's shoulders seemed almost too fragile, too frail, to support the vestment, dragging a little heavily because of the gold-binding, that the same shoulders were the shoulders of a being, an almost disembodied spirit. She constructed perfect and flawless (as in her verse, she carved from current Aeolic dialect, immortal phrases) the whole, the perfection, the undying spirit of goddess, muse or sacred being from the simple grace of some tall, half-developed girl. The very skies open, were opened by these light fingers, fluffing out the under-feathers of the pigeon's throat. Then the wise Sappho clamours aloud against that bitter, bitter creature, Eros, who has once more betrayed her. "Ah, Atthis, you hate even to think of me—you have gone to Andromeda."

I love to think of Atthis and Andromeda curled on a sun-baked marble bench like the familiar Tanagra group, talking it over. What did they say? What did they think? Doubtless, they thought little or nothing and said much.

There is another girl, a little girl. Her name is Cleis. It is reported that the mother of Sappho was named Cleis. It is said that Sappho had a daughter whom she called Cleis.

Cleis was golden. No doubt Cleis was perfect. Cleis was a beautiful baby, looking exactly like a yellow flower (so her mother tells us). She was so extraordinarily beautiful, Lydia had nothing so sweet, so spiced; greatness, wealth, power, nothing in all Lydia could be exchanged for Cleis.

So in the realm of the living, we know there was a Cleis. I see her heaping shells, purple and rose-edged, stained here and there with saffron colours, shells from Adriatic waters heaped in her own little painted bowl and poured out again and gathered up only to be spilt once more across the sands. We have seen Atthis of yester-year; Andromeda of "fair requital," Mnasidika with provoking length of over-shapely limbs; Gyrinno, loved for some appealing gesture or strange resonance of voice or skill of finger-tips, though failing in the essential and more obvious qualities of beauty; Eranna with lips curved contemptuously over slightly irregular though white and perfect teeth; angry Eranna who refused everyone and bound white violets only for the straight hair she herself braided with precision and cruel self-torturing neatness about her own head. We know of Gorgo, over-riotous, too heavy, with special intoxicating sweetness, but exhausting, a girl to weary of, no companion, her over-soft curves presaging early development of heavy womanhood.

Among the living there are these and others. Timas, dead among the living, lying with lily wreath and funeral torch, a golden little bride, lives though sleeping more poignantly even than the famous Graeco-Egyptian beauty the poet's brother married at Naucratis. Rhodope, a name redolent, (even though we may no longer read the tribute of the bridegroom's sister) of the heavy out-curling, over-lapping petals of the peerless flower.

Little—not little—but all, all roses! So at the last, we are forced to accept the often quoted tribute of Meleager, late Alexandrian, half Jew, half Grecian poet. Little but all roses! True, Sappho has become for us a name, an abstraction as well as a pseudonym for poignant human feeling, she is indeed rocks set in a blue sea, she is the sea itself, breaking and tortured and torturing, but never broken. She is the island of artistic perfection where the lover of ancient beauty (shipwrecked in the modern world) may yet find foothold and take breath and gain courage for new adventures and dream of yet unexplored continents and realms of future artistic achievement. She is the wise Sappho.

Plato, poet and philosopher in the most formidable period of Athenian culture, looking back some centuries toward Mitylene, having perspective and a rare standard of comparison, too, speaks of this woman as among the wise.

You were the morning star among the living (the young Plato, poet and Athenian, wrote of a friend he had lost), you were the morning star before you died; now you are "as Hesperus, giving new splendour to the dead." Plato lives as a poet, as a lover, though the Republic seems but a ponderous tome and the mysteries of the Dialogues verge often on the didactic and artificial. So Sappho must live, roses, but many roses, for tradition has set flower upon flower about her name and would continue to do so though her last line were lost.

Perhaps to Meleager, having access to the numberless scrolls of Alexandria, there seemed "but little" though to us, in a cheerless and more barren age, there seems much. Legend upon legend has grown up, adding curious documents to each precious fragment; the history of the preservation of each line is in itself a most fascinating and bewildering romance.

Courtesan and woman of fashion were rebuked at one time for not knowing "even the works of Sappho." Sophocles cried out in despair before some inimitable couplet, "gods—what impassioned heart and longing made this rhythm." The Roman Emperor, weary to

death, left his wreathed drinking cup and said,
"It is worth living yet to hear another of this
woman's songs." Catullus, impassioned lyrist,
left off recounting the imperfections of his Les-
bia to enter a fair paradisal world, to forge
silver Latin from imperishable Greek, to mar-
vel at the praises of this perfect lover who
needed no interim of hatred to repossess the
loved one. Monk and scholar, grey recluse of
Byzantium or Roman or medieval monastery,
flamed to new birth of intellectual passion at
discovery of some fatal relic until the Vatican
itself was moved and deemed this woman fit
rival to the seductions of another Poet and
destroyed her verses.

   The roses Meleager saw as "little" have
become in the history not only of literature but
of nations (Greece and Rome and mediaeval
town and Tuscan city) a great power, roses, but
many, many roses, each fragment witness to
the love of some scholar or hectic antiquary
searching to find a precious inch of palimpsest
among the funereal glories of the sand-strewn
Pharaohs.

GLOSSARY

Eleusinian Mysteries: Every year at Eleusis the Greeks celebrated the rites of Demeter, goddess of the earth and the harvest. These rituals were the most important of the religious calendar, and only initiates were allowed to participate fully in the rites.

Epithets of the Gods: The Greek Gods all had epithets attached to their names which were associated with specific cults:

Zeus Endendros: a cult of Zeus which located the god's shrine in a tree. Zeus was thought to have spoken through the rustling of the leaves.

Zeus Melios: At the beginning of winter a feast of atonement was held, featuring Zeus as a god of the underworld.

Zeus Anthios: With this epithet Dionysius was related to the cult which organized the Dionysian flower festival. The festival was also associated with Demeter and was the prelude to the Eleusinian Mysteries.

Dionysius Zagreus: The cult of Dionysius Zagreus coupled him with violent death and the underworld.

Aphrogenia is an epithet for Aphrodite, meaning "born from the foam."

Kyllenian Hermes refers to Hermes' birth on Mount Kyllene, Arcadia.

Golden Plate: H.D. refers to the "Golden Plate" in Exodus 28, where God instructs Aaron to make a plate of gold, inscribed with the words, "Set Apart for the Lord." In the same section H.D. alludes to the New Testament legend of Christ and the swine of Gadara. According to the Gospels, Christ comes upon a legion of demons in Gadara and casts them into the bodies of swine, who then plunge at full speed into the sea.

Lais: A famous courtesan who was murdered in the temple of Aphrodite (Aphrogenia) by Thessalian women who feared the effect of her beauty on the men of the coast.

Lo-Fu: H.D. refers to a poet, Lo-Fu, living in A.D. 184, Ming Dynasty. In fact, the Ming Dynasty extends from 1368-1664. H.D. might mean the Han Dynasty, and be alluding to the legend of a beautiful woman poet named Lo-Fu. There is no historical reference to a Lo-Fu in the Ming Dynasty.

Meleager of Gadara: A trilingual poet, born in Syria, who lived in Tyre and spoke Greek, Syrian, and Phoenician. *Heliodora* and *Zenophile* were women to whom Meleager wrote poems.

Polycleitus: Greek sculptor of the Fifth Century.

361 A.D.: H.D. mentions the conquest of Delphi by by the Galilean in "the year A.D.361." In A.D.330, Constantinople became the capital of the Roman Empire on the site of Byzantium (which had been founded by citizens from Gadara). When Julian became Emperor in A.D.361, he attempted to rein-stitute polytheism throughout the Empire, but failed.

A.J.